CLEO'S COLOR BOOK

Caroline Mockford

Barefoot Books
Celebrating Art and Story

Cleo is looking at colors today.

Let's see what she learns when she goes out to play.

Here is a bicycle, shiny and red.

Here is a flower with a round yellow head.

Here are some plums,

all
purple
and sweet.

And here's
some pink
ice cream,
delicious
to eat!

Here's a small dog
with a big orange ball.

And here's a
black kitten on
my garden wall.

Here are some
apples, all
crunchy and green.

And here is a bath
and a
blue submarine.

Here is a bear, all cuddly and brown.

And here's the white moon shining over the town.

There are so many colors

that Cleo can see.

Try mixing your own and share them with me!

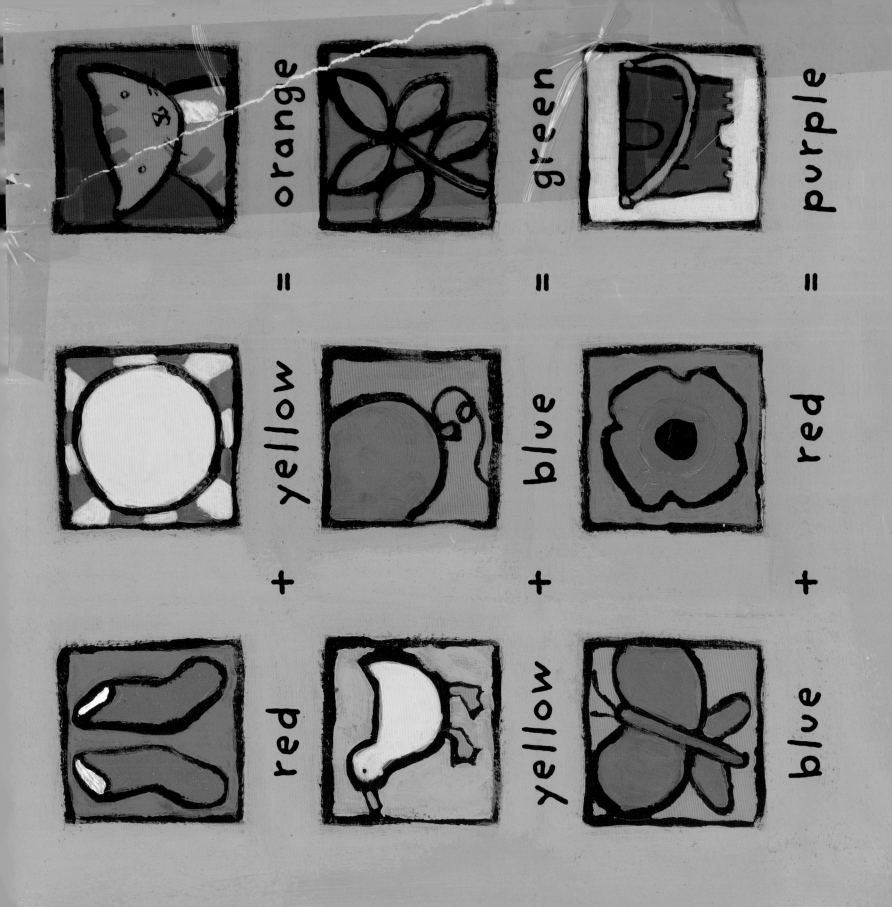

orange = yellow + red

green = blue + yellow

purple = red + blue

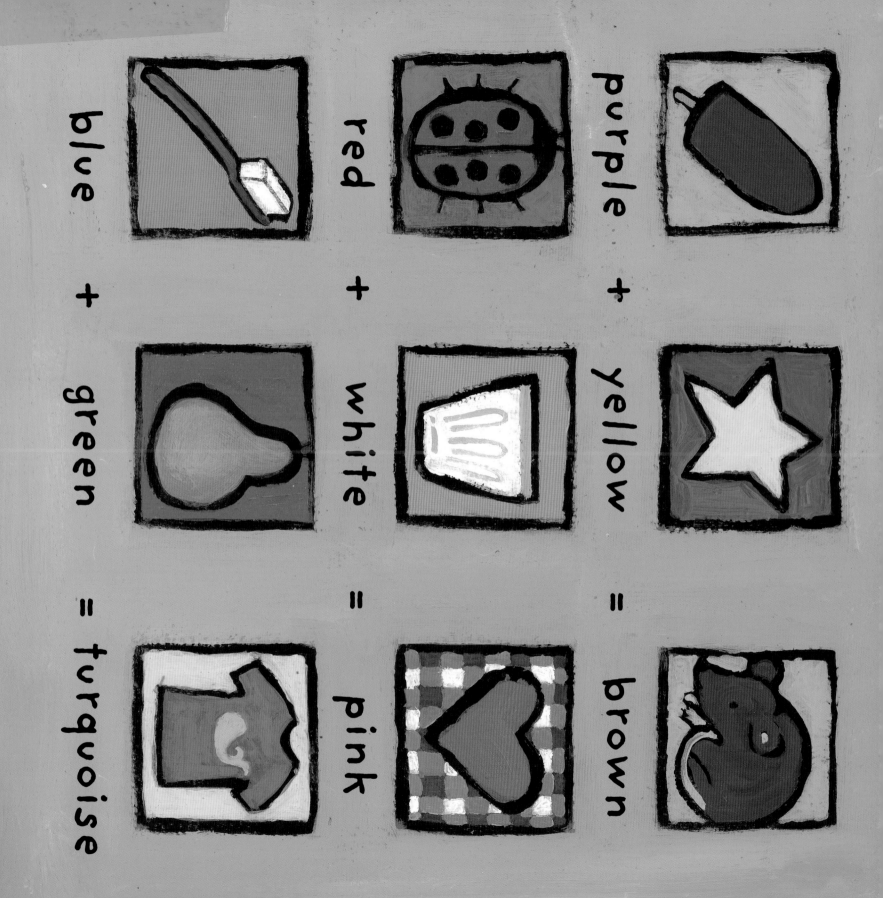

blue + green = turquoise

red + white = pink

purple + yellow = brown

Barefoot Books
2067 Massachusetts Ave
Cambridge, MA 02140

The illustrations were prepared in acrylics on 140lb watercolor paper
Design by Barefoot Books, Bath. Typeset in 44pt Providence Sans Bold
Color separation by Bright Arts, Singapore
Printed and bound in China

3 5 7 9 8 6 4 2

Library of Congress Cataloging-in-Publication Data

Blackstone, Stella.
Cleo's color book / Stella Blackstone ; [illustrations by] Caroline Mockford.
p. cm.
Summary: When Cleo the cat goes out to play, she observes a variety of colors in the things around
her.
ISBN 1-905236-30-1 (hardcover : alk. paper) [1. Color--Fiction. 2. Cats--Fiction. 3. Stories in rhyme.]
I. Mockford, Caroline, ill. II. Title.

PZ8.3.B5735Cld 2006
[E]--dc22

Barefoot Books
Celebrating Art and Story

At Barefoot Books, we celebrate art and story that opens
the hearts and minds of children from all walks of life, inspiring
them to read deeper, search further, and explore their own creative gifts.
Taking our inspiration from many different cultures, we focus on themes that
encourage independence of spirit, enthusiasm for learning, and sharing of
the world's diversity. Interactive, playful and beautiful, our products
combine the best of the present with the best of the past to
educate our children as the caretakers of tomorrow.

www.barefootbooks.com

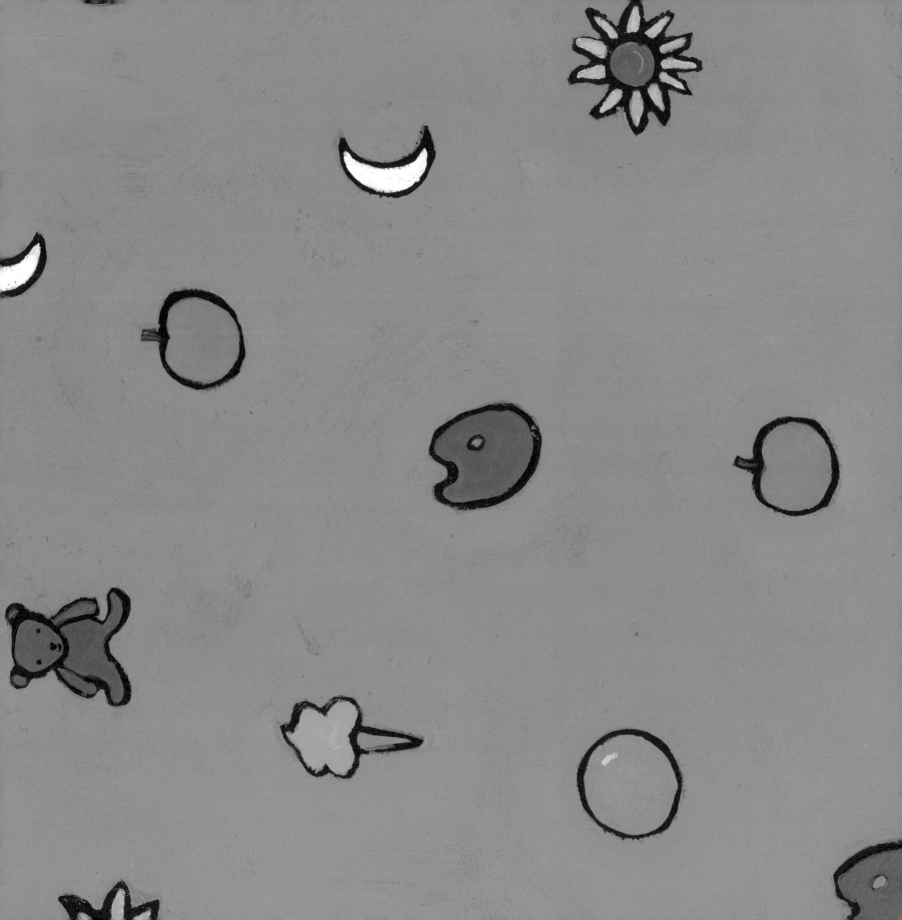